For Molly Melling
Thanks Mum

JUST LIKE MY MUM
by David Melling

First published in 2004
by Hodder Children's Books

This edition published in 2008

Hodder Children's Books
338 Euston Road
London NW1 3BH

Hodder Children's Books Australia
Level 17/207 Kent Street
Sydney, NSW 2000

ISBN: 978 0 340 94416 5
10 9 8 7 6 5 4

Printed in China

Hodder Children's Books is a division of Hachette Children's Books
An Hachette Livre UK Company
www.hachettelivre.co.uk

Just Like My Mum

David Melling

Hodder
Children's
Books

A division of Hachette Children's Books

This is my mum.

In the morning I always wake early...

…just like my mum.

I y-a-w-n,

and g*rrr*oan,

and I'm ready
for the day...

...just like my mum.

If I hurt myself,

or argue with someone,

or get upset...

...my mum makes me feel better.

And when
I'm a cheeky
little monkey…

I say 'sorry'…

…just like my mum.

When I'm bored my mum
doesn't like it.

She says,

'Why don't you *do* something?'

But when I do something...

she says,

'Just sit still
for five
minutes!'

My mum helps
me make things.
She knows
everything.

And her ideas are *so* interesting…

...*everyone* wants to play!

Sometimes I have good
ideas of my own…

But Mum says,
        'Dry games are better!'

                        That's typical…

...just like
   my mum.

There's an old squiggly
tree which is my
favourite place
for climbing with
my friends.

At the end of the day,
we all want to be somewhere
quiet, safe and warm,
with someone…

...just like
my mum.

Other books by David Melling:

The Kiss That Missed

Good Knight, Sleep Tight

The Three Wishes

Two by Two and a Half

The Scallywags

The Tale of Jack Frost

The Ghost Library

Just Like My Dad